UPSY DOWN
TOWN

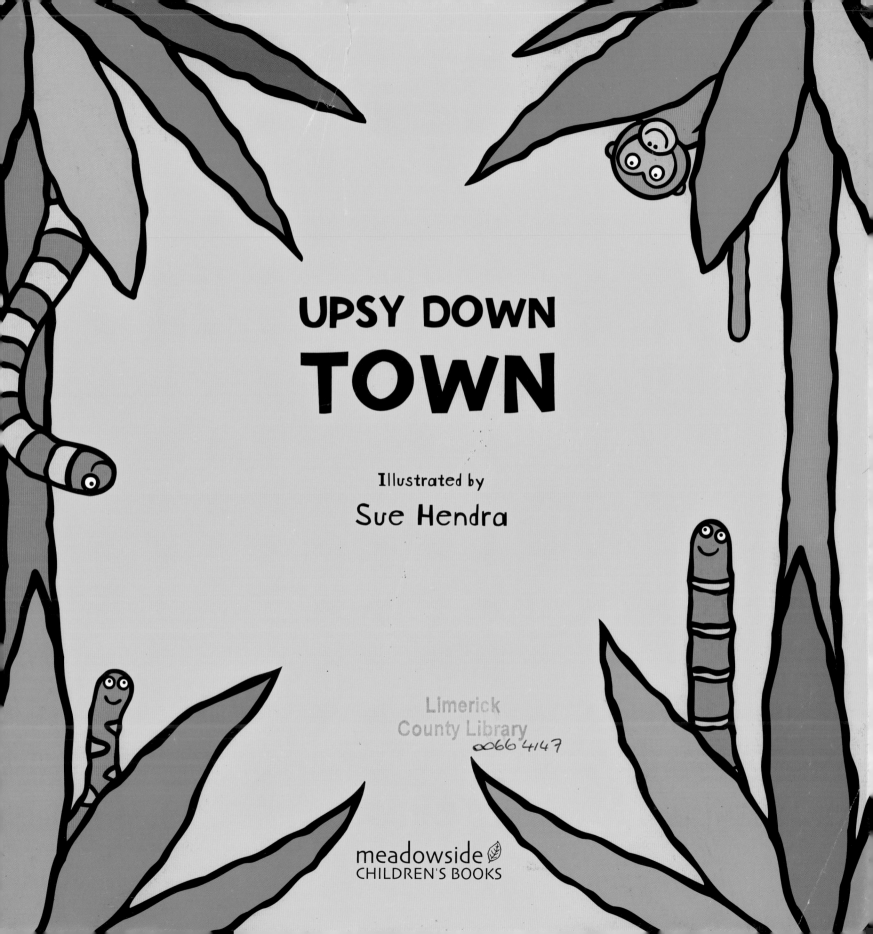

UPSY DOWN
TOWN

Illustrated by

Sue Hendra

meadowside
CHILDREN'S BOOKS

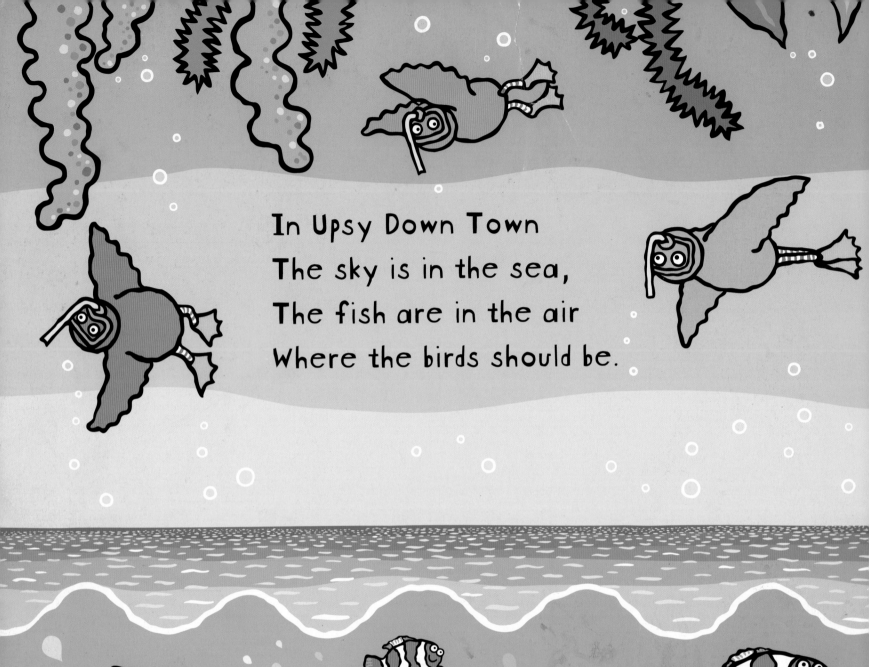

In Upsy Down Town
The sky is in the sea,
The fish are in the air
Where the birds should be.

The rain is falling up,
Instead of falling down,
In the world of Upsy Down Town.

In Upsy Down Town
The sheep are in the trees,
Cows hang off the branches
Where the birds should be.
You walk upon your nose,
Instead of on your toes,
In the world of Upsy Down Town.

In Upsy Down Town
A monkey's in the nest,
Telling funny stories
So the birds can't rest.
No one knows why
There's a tiger flying by,
In the world of Upsy Down Town.

In Upsy Down Town
There's a hippo in the sky,
Giraffes in the clouds
Where the birds should fly.
A chicken flies the planes
While a walrus drives the trains,
In the world of Upsy Down Town.

In Upsy Down Town
The elephants are thin,
Nothing's as it should be
So the birds can't win.

With bananas in the air,
No one seems to care,
In the world of Upsy Down Town.

In Upsy Down Town
The birds begin to hop,
The rabbits start to fly,
Then the birds shout...

Everything is on its head.
Turn the book around instead!

In Downy Up Town
The sea is down below,
The clouds are in the sky,
The fish know where to go.

The birds are in their nest.
They really need the rest.
Goodnight in Downy Up Town.

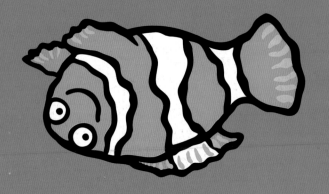

for **Ella, Louie and Mae**

S.H

First published in 2004
by Meadowside Children's Books
185 Fleet Street,
London EC4A 2HS

Text © Beth Shoshan 2004, based on a traditional nursery rhyme
Illustrations © Sue Hendra 2004
The rights of Beth Shoshan and Sue Hendra to be identified
as the author and illustrator of this work have been asserted by
them in accordance with the Copyright, Designs and Patents Act, 1988

10 9 8 7 6 5 4 3